Contents

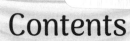

Bridesmaids Club

Big Bollywood Wedding

Posy Diamond

With special thanks to Linda Chapman.
With thanks to Inclusive Minds for connecting us with their
Inclusion Ambassador network,
in particular Ishani Shah for her input.
Thanks also to Namishka Doshi for her help.

ORCHARD BOOKS

First published in Great Britain in 2020 by The Watts Publishing Group

1 3 5 7 9 10 8 6 4 2

Text copyright © Orchard Books 2020
Illustrations copyright © Orchard Books 2020
The moral rights of the author and illustrator have been waived.

A CIP catalogue record for this book
is available from the British Library.

ISBN 978 1 40836 094 1

Printed and bound in Great Britain by Clays Ltd, Elcograf S.p.A

The paper and board used in this book are made from wood from responsible sources.

Orchard Books
An imprint of
Hachette Children's Group
Part of The Watts Publishing Group Limited
Carmelite House
50 Victoria Embankment
London EC4Y 0DZ

An Hachette UK Company
www.hachette.co.uk
www.hachettechildrens.co.uk

Chapter One

"This reminds me of your mum and dad's wedding, Sophie!" said Shanti, dancing round her small bedroom with her three friends. "Do you remember? We danced to this song."

"I can't believe it was a month ago now," said Sophie, her blonde ponytail

bouncing as she spun. "It feels like just last week."

"It was an awesome day!" said Cora.

"Look – here we are," said Emily, pulling out her phone and showing them her screensaver. It was a photo of the four friends standing on the beach at the wedding, arms round each other, beaming at the camera.

Shanti smiled as she remembered the day – the pavilion decked out with fairy lights, Sophie's mum in her beautiful dress, the delicious pizza and ice cream at Franketelli's Italian restaurant afterwards – and then dancing long into the night. "It was a perfect wedding!"

"And it wouldn't have happened without Bridesmaids Club," said Sophie.

"We rock!" Cora agreed as Sophie high-fived her friends.

They went to the same large primary school, but they hadn't known each other very well until a few months ago when they had discovered they were all going to be bridesmaids. They had started the Bridesmaids Club so that they could help make the four weddings they were involved in go perfectly. However, they'd had no idea that they would end up organising a whole wedding for Sophie's parents.

When Sophie's dad had lost his job, he

and Sophie's mum had decided to cancel
the tropical wedding they had planned
and it had looked like Sophie might
not be a bridesmaid at all. But then the
Bridesmaids Club had come up with the
plan of organising a surprise wedding
on the local beach. With some help from
Sophie's aunt, they'd actually pulled it
off! It had been a real challenge but so
much fun.

"So, I've been a bridesmaid, it's your
turn next," Sophie said to Shanti.

"It's just a week now until Rekha's
wedding, isn't it?" said Emily.

Shanti nodded. Rekha was her older
sister and the wedding celebrations were

starting on Saturday – in six days' time. She looked over at the beautiful pink bridesmaid lehenga hanging on her wardrobe door. "I can't wait. It's going to be so much fun," she said, her brown eyes shining.

"What happens at an Indian wedding?" asked Cora curiously.

"Well, I've only been to one and that was when I was little so I don't really remember it very well," admitted Shanti. Her mum's

family was originally from northern India. Her mum had grown up there and come over to England when she was eighteen, but her dad had been born in the UK. Shanti had been very surprised when her sister had said she wanted to have a big Indian wedding, but her husband-to-be, Ansh, came from a much more traditional family.

"It's not just one ceremony, like at Sophie's mum and dad's wedding," Shanti went on. "There are lots of different celebrations. We've already had a big engagement party at Ansh's house. For the wedding itself, there'll be several ceremonies and lots of eating, dancing

and partying for three days. We've got relatives coming from all over the place. Nani – that's my mum's mother – is coming from India. She's arriving tonight and staying here until after the wedding. Mum's really stressing out about it because she hasn't been to visit since I was three. Mum says Nani's very traditional and we're just not. I hope it's OK."

"That must be weird not to see your grandma often," said Sophie. "I see my gran every week."

Shanti shrugged. "I'm used to it. I've got lots of other relatives I see – aunties, uncles and cousins. We do

sometimes Skype her. She just doesn't like travelling."

"It sounds like there's going to be loads to do for the wedding," said Emily. "If there's anything the Bridesmaids Club can help with, then let us know."

"Well, actually, there is something . . ." Shanti admitted.

"What?' asked Cora curiously.

"It's only a small thing," said Shanti. "But I can't work out what to get Rekha as a wedding present. I want to get her something special," she continued, feeling a warm glow as she thought about her sister. Rekha was twenty-one, ten years older than Shanti, but she was the best big sister in the world. She was always ready to listen when Shanti wanted to talk. She helped Shanti with her homework and they went clothes shopping together at least once a month – and Rekha always treated her! Shanti knew she was going to really miss Rekha when she moved out to live with Ansh, after the wedding. She looked hopefully at her friends. "Any ideas for what I could get her?"

"You could buy some nice jewellery," suggested Cora. "Then when she wears it, it'll remind her of you."

"I could but I haven't got enough money," Shanti said.

"Then why don't you make her something?" suggested Sophie.

Emily nodded. "Home-made things are just as nice as shop-bought things. Better, even, because they show you really care."

Shanti frowned doubtfully. "I'm not great at making things."

"We can help you," said Emily eagerly. "I'm sure I can find something in one of my dad's books." Her dad ran a craft shop and Emily shared his love of painting, drawing and making things. "I'll have a look and find some ideas."

Shanti beamed. "Thanks!"

"And let us know if there's anything else that needs doing for the wedding,"

said Sophie. "Anything. After all, that's what the Bridesmaids Club is for!" She jumped to her feet. "Now let's dance some more!"

Sophie pulled the others to their feet. Soon they were dancing round Shanti's bedroom, even though there wasn't much space. As Shanti spun round with the others and lost herself in the music, she

felt a tingly rush of happiness. She had a wedding to look forward to, a beautiful bridesmaid outfit to wear and the best friends in the whole world!

Chapter Two

"Have you come to catch up on *Dance Off?*" said Rekha when Shanti went to her sister's bedroom after the rest of the Bridesmaids Club had gone home.

"Yep," said Shanti happily. *Dance Off* was their favourite TV programme. The contestants had to learn different types

of dance each week. Shanti and Rekha both loved dancing. Shanti did ballet and tap, and Rekha went to Indian dance classes, which was where she had met her fiancé, Ansh.

Every week, Shanti and her sister snuggled up on Rekha's bed and watched *Dance Off* together. If they couldn't watch it live, they always watched it on catch up. Rekha turned her television on but as she did so her mobile rang.

"It's Ansh," Rekha said, looking at the screen. "He's video calling." She answered the call. "Hi, babe."

Shanti moved so she could see over

Rekha's shoulder. Ansh's handsome face filled the screen, his dark hair falling over his forehead. "Hi, Ansh!" she called, waving.

He grinned and waved back. "Hey, Shanti," he whispered.

Shanti frowned. It looked like Ansh was in the dark. "Where are you? And why are you whispering?"

Ansh's eyes darted furtively from side to side. "I'm in my bedroom with the light switched off. I don't want anyone to know I'm in here!"

"Why?" asked Rekha.

"I'm hiding from my aunties." Ansh shook his head. "Three of them are

staying at our house from now until the wedding. They're driving me nuts. They keep telling me what a fine boy I am and ruffling my hair—"

"It *is* very nice hair," Rekha put in, smiling.

"Well, I wouldn't mind you ruffling it," said Ansh, with a cheeky twinkle in his eye. He shook his head in mock dismay. "Oh, Rekha, what have we got ourselves into?"

Rekha grinned. "I told you we should have just had a simple registry office wedding. But no, you were the one who wanted the whole big wedding with all the relatives and all the fuss—"

Ansh interrupted her. "Oh, help, they're coming! They've found me!" There was the sound of a door opening and Shanti heard the chatter of excited voices.

"Here he is! Our handsome nephew!"

"Hiding like a little mouse in the dark! Who would believe it?"

"Gotta go!" hissed Ansh, ending the call.

Shanti giggled. "Poor Ansh!"

"It's his own fault," said Rekha, putting her phone on her bedside table. "He wanted all this – the ceremonies, the food, the guests, the wedding clothes. He's more of a bridezilla than I am! He even wants to know what mehndi

patterns I've chosen for my hands and feet."

"Have you decided yet?' Shanti asked curiously. At the mehndi ceremony, Rekha would have her hands and feet decorated with delicate patterns painted in henna, a dark paste made from plants.

"Not yet," said Rekha with a shrug. "I really don't know whether to go for traditional or modern patterns. Do you want to have a look with me? After all, you need to choose what you want on your hands too."

"OK, let's look," said Shanti eagerly. As bridesmaid she was going to have mehndi too! Rekha got out her iPad

and they sat on her bed looking at lots
of different photographs of mehndi on
the internet. Some were a traditional
swirling paisley-type pattern, others had
pictures of flowers and birds. Some went
all the way up to the bride's elbows,
while others were just on the hands and
wrists.

"I'd like to have something that has

meaning to me." Rekha pointed to an image which had a football in it. "Maybe I could have a netball!" she joked. She played the position of goal shooter in a women's netball team. "Or some musical notes."

Shanti giggled and nudged her sister. "Maybe you could have a shopping bag or credit card too."

"I don't like to shop that much!" Rekha protested.

Shanti's eyes twinkled. "Really?"

Rekha chuckled. "OK, OK, I do but I'm not having a shopping bag in my wedding mehndi! Nani's so traditional, she would have a fit! One thing I am

definitely going to do is have Ansh's initials hidden in tiny letters in the pattern somewhere and I'll make him find them!" She smiled, her eyes growing dreamy. "Oh, Shanti, I'm so glad I'm marrying Ansh. He's just perfect!"

"He is," Shanti agreed. But even as she smiled at her sister, she had to fight back a wave of sadness. She was very excited about being a bridesmaid, but it wouldn't be the same after the wedding. The house would feel strange once Rekha moved out. "You . . . you'll still come back here and visit us lots, won't you?"

Rekha took her hand and gave it a

squeeze. "Of course I will!" Her eyes searched Shanti's. "Oh, Shanti, you look really upset. Please don't be. I won't be able to be happy on my wedding day unless you're happy too."

Shanti forced a smile. "Of course I'll be happy!"

Just then, there was a knock on the bedroom door. It opened and their dad poked his head round it. "Girls, I've got to go and collect Nani from the airport. Could you give Mum a hand? She's getting very stressed that the house isn't going to be ready."

"Don't worry. We'll come down and help," said Rekha, jumping up.

Shanti followed Rekha and her dad downstairs. *I've got to try and be happy at the wedding,* she thought firmly, remembering the concern in Rekha's eyes. *I'm her bridesmaid and it's my job to make absolutely sure it's the very best day of her life!*

Chapter Three

Shanti could hear her mum clattering around in the kitchen. The hoover was in the middle of the hall floor and a feather duster was lying on top of the hall table. Passing the dining room, Shanti saw that the doors of the polished wood cabinet where they kept the smart china

were open and serving dishes and plates were piled high on the dining table. She followed her dad and Rekha into the kitchen, where Mum was washing up and the kitchen units were covered with baking trays, cooking ingredients, bags of spices and bowls.

Dad glanced at Rekha and Shanti. "HELP!" he mouthed, rolling his eyes at them.

Mum glanced round. "What am I going to do? I'm never going to be ready for Nani! I've still got to cook supper, make some barfi, set the table and finish tidying the house!"

"Don't worry, Mum. We'll help," said

Rekha. "You concentrate on supper. Shanti and I will get everything else ready."

Rekha went to the sink and took over the washing up while Shanti started to sweep the floor.

"I'll set off to the airport then," said Dad, moving away from the chaos.

"Drive back very slowly!" Mum told him.

"I'll take the scenic route and show her the sea and the promenade. Maybe even stop for an ice cream at Franketelli's," said Dad.

"Good plan," said Mum. As Dad left, she groaned. "I do hope this visit goes

well and Nani enjoys her stay."

"I'm sure she will," said Rekha. "When I went to stay with Nani last summer, she was really nice."

"Mmm," said Mum, still sounding worried. "She is very traditional though and has strong ideas about how things should be done. I'm sure she won't think I'm doing them right!"

"Don't worry, Mum," said Shanti, putting away the broom and giving her a hug. "It will be

lovely to have Nani to stay for a while
and I bet she'll be really happy to see
you. I'll go and sort the dining room
out, then I can help make the barfi."
Barfi was a fudge-like sweet that was
apparently Nani's favourite treat.

Shanti shook her head as she went
into the dining room. It was strange to
see her mum, who worked as an office
manager and was usually very calm and
organised, getting so worked up.

I wonder what Nani's like, thought
Shanti, glancing at a photo on the wall.
It was from the last time Nani had
visited England, when Shanti was only
three years old. In the photo, Nani was

sitting on a chair in a cobalt blue sari. She had a slight smile on her face but somehow still looked quite stern. Shanti was sitting on her lap, wearing a very pretty, long silk dress and with her dark hair in two small bunches. *I can't remember that visit at all,* Shanti thought. *It's going to be exciting to see her again and hear about India.* She hoped that one day she'd be able to visit Nani in India like Rekha had the previous summer.

Shanti cleared the table and put on the freshly ironed tablecloth, then set the plates out.

"Good news!" Mum said, poking her head round the door. "Dad's texted. The

plane's been delayed. We've got an extra two hours!"

By the time they heard Dad's key in the front door, they were ready. The whole house had been hoovered and dusted, every pot and pan washed up and tidied away. The barfi was in a tin for later and the lamb biryani that they'd be having for supper was cooking on the hob, making the kitchen smell delicious. Rekha had changed into an orange-and-pink sari that she had bought in India on her visit.

"Everyone, quick! They're here!" said Mum. They all dashed into the hall, plastering big smiles on their faces as the

door opened and Nani came in. Shanti's first thought was: *Wow! She's really small!*

Nani was only a little bit taller than she was, but she had a fierce look about her bird-like face. She was wearing a mustard yellow sari with gold embroidery and had a cardigan over it. Her dark brown eyes were hooded and they flicked from side to side, not seeming to miss a thing. Shanti hung back, feeling suddenly awkward.

"*Maa!*" said Mum, with a warm smile. She gave her mother a hug. "I hope the journey was OK."

"Too long, Ramnik," said Nani, shaking her head.

"Well, at least you're here now, Nani!" said Rekha, hurrying forward.

Nani embraced her. "Ah, Rekha." Her face softened with a smile and she stroked Rekha's cheek. "And how is our bride-to-be feeling?"

"Excited and a bit nervous," admitted Rekha.

"Good, good. Well, I have brought some creams with me to make you extra pretty." She released Rekha and her eyes fell on Shanti.

"Hi, Nani," said Shanti shyly as her grandmother looked her up and down.

Nani waved her hand at Shanti's jeans. "Why is my youngest granddaughter

dressed like a
boy, Ramnik?"

Shanti glanced
at Mum and
Dad, not
knowing what
to say.

"Those are
Shanti's normal clothes, Nani," Mum
said, giving Shanti a reassuring look. "It's
what all the kids wear here."

Nani snorted. "It is lucky I have
bought her some beautiful salwar
kameez to wear, then. You will like that,
Shanti, yes?"

"Um, yes," said Shanti politely,

although she never usually wore
traditional Indian clothes. She realised
Nani was waiting for something more.
"Thank you, Nani."

Nani gave a sniff.

"Come along in, Maa, and I'll get
you some chai. Or maybe you'd prefer a
lassi?" said Mum.

Nani's eyebrows raised. "You know I
never drink lassi after lunch, Ramnik. It
disagrees with me."

"OK, well, chai it is then," said Mum
brightly but as she turned away, Shanti
saw her take a deep breath.

"I'll give you a hand, Mum," she
offered, slipping her hand into her mum's.

"Thanks, sweetie," Mum said, squeezing her fingers.

"I'll show Nani to her bedroom," said Rekha.

"And I'll bring up the cases," said Dad.

In the kitchen, Shanti's mum started making chai – tea with spices and milk.

"I don't think Nani likes my jeans much," sighed Shanti, helping her. "Do I really have to wear the salwar kameez she's bought?"

"Not if you don't want to. And don't worry, Nani's just old-fashioned and probably feeling a bit grumpy because she's had a long flight," said Mum as Shanti got out the pretty blue-and-gold

teacups and saucers that were kept for special occasions.

Shanti nodded but she felt a bit deflated. She'd been looking forward to meeting Nani and she had a feeling that she'd already somehow disappointed her.

Mum saw her face. "She'll be fine once she's unpacked and had a cup of tea," she said reassuringly. "You'll see."

However, as the evening went on, Shanti couldn't seem to do anything right. First, Nani criticised her for not handing the dishes of food round in the correct order.

Then, when they started to eat and
Shanti tried to join in with the wedding
talk, Nani told her not to interrupt.

"Let your sister talk, Shanti! She is the
one getting married."

Shanti subsided into silence. Rekha
gave her a sympathetic look.

When Rekha went out to the kitchen
to help Mum bring in some more dishes,
Nani turned to Shanti. "So, how are you
doing at school, Shanti? What are your
favourite subjects?"

"I like all my subjects," Shanti said.

"Speak up, child!" Nani scolded. "I
cannot hear you when you whisper like
a mouse! What did you say?"

"That I like all my subjects, Nani," said Shanti, trying to speak more loudly.

"Now you are shouting!" Nani exclaimed.

"Why don't you go and help Mum, sweetheart," said Dad. Shanti jumped to her feet and escaped gratefully.

After supper, Nani fetched the salwar kameez she'd bought for Shanti to wear – long tunics and baggy trousers that came in at the ankle. They were very pretty colours and the fabric was soft and silky. She thanked Nani but she didn't offer to try them on. From Nani's expression she felt like she had disappointed her again.

Rekha brought down her beautiful red-and-gold wedding lehenga so Nani could see it. Nani exclaimed happily as she inspected it. "It is very fine. You will be a beautiful bride."

"Shanti will look beautiful in her lehenga too," said Rekha. "She's going to be my bridesmaid."

"Bridesmaid! Pfff!" Nani snorted. "In my day we didn't have *bridesmaids*."

"Nani!" Rekha said. "Don't be old-fashioned. Lots of Indian weddings have bridesmaids these days."

Nani sniffed and pulled some old black-and-white photos out of her bag. "Now, this is what a wedding should be

45

like. This is your *dada ji* arriving on an elephant when he and I got married," she was saying as she passed one of the photos to Rekha.

"Oh, wow!" said Rekha. "Look, Shanti. This is our grandfather."

"Be careful! No sticky fingers, Shanti!" Nani said as if Shanti was a little child.

Shanti wiped her fingers obediently and took the old photograph carefully. She looked at the handsome, young man in a turban riding on the back of an elephant surrounded by a large group of friends and family. It was hard to believe that she was looking at their grandfather, who had died a long time ago. She shot

a grin at Rekha. "Imagine if Ansh showed up on an elephant at your wedding! That would be so funny!"

"Tradition should not be laughed at, Shanti!" Nani snapped.

Shanti's cheeks burned. She was beginning to feel like whatever she said or did was wrong.

Mum gave her a sympathetic look. "Why don't you pop into the kitchen, Shanti, and get some of the barfi you made? It's delicious," she said, turning to Nani. "Shanti's good at baking."

Shanti sighed as she put the diamond-shaped barfi out on a plate. She'd been looking forward to meeting Nani, but it wasn't turning out like she'd imagined. Mum had said that Nani was just grumpy because she was tired from travelling, but that clearly wasn't true. Nani was fine with Rekha, all smiles and compliments. *It's just me she's being grumpy with,* Shanti thought unhappily. *She doesn't seem to like me at all!*

Chapter Four

"You won't believe what Horrible Helena's done now!" Cora exclaimed, rolling her eyes as the four friends in the Bridesmaids Club had lunch together the next day at school.

"What?' said Shanti, biting into an apple. Horrible Helena was Cora's dad's

fiancée. They were getting married soon and Cora was not happy about it!

"Well, she bought me a dress!" Cora said, looking as outraged as if Helena had given her a squashed frog.

Emily frowned. "What's the problem with that?"

"I don't wear dresses. You know I don't," exclaimed Cora. "Helena should know that too but no, she came in from shopping and handed me this big bag. I thought it might be a pair of jeans or a t-shirt but no, it was a sparkly dress. *A dress!*"

Sophie grinned. "Stop being such a drama queen, Cora! I'm sure Helena

was only trying to be nice."

"Yes, she probably assumed you like dresses because Mollie May does," Shanti chipped in. Helena had a five-year-old daughter who liked everything pink and sparkly.

"Ugh!" Cora said, with a scowl. "Mollie May is such a spoiled brat."

Shanti quickly changed the subject. "Hey, Emily, did you come up with any ideas for something I can make for Rekha?" she asked. "I'm going to have to get on with it. There are only a few days left until the wedding celebrations begin."

"I had homework to do last night so

I didn't have time to look through the magazines," admitted Emily. "But I asked my dad this morning and he suggested making up a photo album or scrapbook with lots of pictures of you and Rekha together?"

"I guess I could, but she already has a photo collage of us up on her wall," said Shanti. "She's taking it with her when she and Ansh move in together."

"Could you bake her something?' suggested Sophie. "A special cake maybe?"

Shanti felt doubtful. "There's going to be so much food at the wedding. I don't think she'll want anything else to eat . . ."

"Could you take her out for the day?" said Cora. "You could do something fun together – like come to the riding stables I go to and go out for a hack together."

"Ooh, yes!" said Emily.

"It's a really nice idea but riding would cost money, wouldn't it?" said Shanti.

Cora nodded.

"Well, how about just going for a walk somewhere special one day after school?" suggested Sophie. "Somewhere you used to go when you were little. You could take a picnic."

"That would be perfect," Shanti agreed, "but I know I won't be able to get her away from the wedding

preparations. There's going to be so much going on at home this week."

When Shanti had left to go to school that morning, Nani had been sitting at the kitchen table with Rekha, talking through the arrangements for all the celebrations that were going to take place. "My Auntie Nisha's coming round this afternoon and tomorrow Ansh is coming over. There'll be lots and lots of cooking and then on Saturday everything starts properly. The thing I'm looking forward to most is the sangeet."

"What's that?" asked Emily curiously.

"It's a big party with lots of food, singing and dancing for both families. It's

happening at our house on Saturday, the night before the wedding."

"It sounds amazing!" said Sophie.

"I wish we could come," said Cora longingly.

"I'll ask if you can," said Shanti. "There are going to be loads of people there, so a few more probably won't matter."

"I'd love to come if it's OK with your parents and Rekha," said Emily and the other two nodded.

"It sounds like you haven't got a chance of getting Rekha away on her own for some special sister bonding time though," said Sophie.

Shanti shook her head. "No, I'm going to have to think of something else as a present."

"I'll check those craft magazines tonight," Emily promised.

"Thanks," said Shanti. She hesitated, wondering whether to confide in her friends about the other thing that was bothering her. "I've kind of got another problem too," she admitted.

"What?" asked Emily.

Shanti took a breath. "It's Nani," she said. "She arrived yesterday and well . . . I don't think she likes me." She chewed a fingernail and glanced anxiously at her friends.

"What do you mean, she doesn't like you?" said Sophie.

"She was very snappy with me yesterday,' said Shanti. "She was all smiles with Rekha, but she kept telling me off." She explained what had happened the night before. "I just got the feeling I disappointed her."

Sophie hugged her. "I'm sure that's not true. She's your grandma. She loves you."

"I guess," said Shanti. She hadn't felt as though Nani even *liked* her.

"Maybe she was just tired?" suggested Emily.

"That's what Mum said, but then why was she fine with Rekha and not me?"

Sophie, Cora and Emily looked at each other. None of them seemed to have an answer.

"I'm sure it'll improve," said Sophie encouragingly. "After all, you haven't seen her since you were little and you can be kind of quiet and shy at times. You probably just need time to get to know each other."

"Yeah, she knows Rekha better than you," said Emily.

"I'm sure by the wedding everything will be fine!" said Cora optimistically.

Shanti nodded slowly. She hoped her friends were right!

Chapter Five

Shanti hurried home that afternoon.
Her house was quite close to the school
and now that she was in Year Six, her
parents allowed her to walk to and from
school on her own – though they still
gave her a lift in the car when it was
raining! Excitement fizzed through her. It

would be lovely to see Auntie Nisha and her three little cousins, and she wanted to find out what wedding preparations had been going on that day. She bet they'd done a lot of cooking! It was also her special TV night with Rekha. Every Monday, when they could, Shanti and Rekha watched *Dance Off*.

It suddenly dawned on Shanti that this would be the last time they watched it together. Her excitement faded. This time next week, Rekha would be married and she would have moved out of the family home.

I'm going to miss her so much, she thought, her heart twisting. She wanted

Rekha to get married and be happy, she really did, and she was looking forward to being a bridesmaid so much. But after the wedding everything would be different.

It'll be just me and Mum and Dad from next week. Shanti tried to fight back the feeling that she didn't want things to change. *I want Rekha to be happy,* she told herself firmly. *Even if it makes me sad.*

She stopped at the corner shop and bought a bag of crisps with her pocket money. Munching on them, she turned into their driveway. Their house was on a modern housing estate. It had a paved drive and a neat front garden bordered

by a low hedge. Shanti used her key to let herself in. As she stepped into the hall, she breathed in the smell of sugar and cardamom. The TV was on in the lounge but she dumped her bag on the floor and headed into the kitchen, where she could hear the voices of her mum, Nani and Auntie Nisha.

"Wow!" she said as she walked in. Every surface was covered with delicious-looking Indian sweets. Shanti's mouth watered.

"Hey, it's Shanti!" said Auntie Nisha, coming over to greet her with a hug and a kiss. She wasn't actually a real aunt; she was Mum's cousin, but Shanti had

always called her 'auntie'. She had three daughters – seven-year-old Pari, six-year-old Anvi and two-year-old Shreya.

"Hi, Auntie Nisha," said Shanti, hugging her back. "It looks like it's been busy here."

"We've been cooking all day!" said Rekha, carrying a big bowl filled with soft, white spongy balls of rasgulla to the utility room, where there was an extra fridge. "Nani's been brilliant," she said, throwing a smile at her grandmother. "She's so good at making things."

Nani looked pleased. "In my time we learnt how to do things properly. None of these modern short cuts." She pointed

dismissively at the microwave and then frowned at Shanti. "What are you eating, Shanti?"

"Salt and vinegar crisps," said Shanti. She offered Nani the pack. "Would you like one?"

Nani waved the pack away. "Crisps! You should have waited until you got back and had one of my samosas."

"But I like crisps, Nani," said Shanti. "I like Indian food too," she added hastily as Nani started to frown. "But I was hungry and wanted something to eat on the walk home from school."

"Right, well, I've got to get supper on so don't eat anything else or you'll spoil

your appetite," said Mum quickly. "Aloo Gobi and roti tonight. The cauliflower and potatoes are prepared but I still need to cook them. We'll eat at seven-thirty."

Shanti felt her heart sink. "But that's when Rekha and I watch *Dance Off*, Mum!"

Nani frowned. "Shanti, you should be asking your mother what you can do to help with the cooking, not worrying about a TV programme. *Tsk*."

Shanti felt bad. Normally she would have offered to help, but it was the last time she and Rekha would ever watch *Dance Off* together. She would have explained but she didn't want to say

anything in front of Rekha – she didn't want her sister to know how sad she was feeling about her moving out, and all their little routines, like watching TV and shopping together, changing.

"I couldn't have watched it anyway tonight, Shanti," Rekha said quickly, coming back into the kitchen from the utility room. "There's so much still to sort out for the wedding."

"Yes, many, many things," said Nani, wiping her floury hands on a tea towel. "What are you planning for the sangeet, Rekha? What music? What entertainment?"

"Er, I'm not completely sure," said

Rekha, looking flustered. "I hadn't really thought about entertainment."

"There must be entertainment," said Nani firmly. "Or your guests will be disappointed."

"Can I help with anything?" Shanti said, going over to Rekha.

"No. No." Nani waved her away impatiently with a hand. "Do not bother your sister now."

"But I'm the bridesmaid," Shanti protested. "I'm not bothering her. I want to help."

Nani's eyebrows shot up.

Rekha opened her mouth to say something, but just then Auntie Nisha

spoke. "Shanti, why don't you go and play with the little ones?" she said quickly. "They'll probably be getting bored of watching the TV now."

"Yes, if you could keep them company that would be very helpful," Mum put in.

Angry words rose up inside Shanti. She didn't want to go and play with her cousins. She wanted to help Rekha. But she didn't want to cause trouble so she bit her protest back. "OK," she sighed. As she reached the door, she remembered something. "Mum, can Cora, Emily and Sophie come to the sangeet? None of them know what an Indian wedding is like and they're really interested."

"Of course they can come," Rekha said quickly. "That's fine, isn't it, Mum? They can come to the mehndi too – and the wedding, if they want."

Mum smiled. "Three more people is certainly not going to make any difference to the celebrations. Tell them they're very welcome to come to any part of it. We'd love them to be there."

Feeling a bit happier, Shanti grinned. "Thanks!"

She went into the lounge, where her little cousins were watching *Beauty and the Beast*. As soon as they saw her, they squealed and ran over.

"Danti! Danti!" chanted Shreya, the

youngest, hugging her legs.

"Will you watch the movie with us, Shanti?" asked Anvi.

"Can we do your hair?" asked Pari, stroking Shanti's long, dark hair.

"OK," said Shanti, sitting down on the sofa. Shreya climbed on to her lap while Anvi and Pari combed out her hair with their fingers and each made a plait. Shanti started to watch the film. It was

the big dance scene near the end of the
movie. Hearing the music, Shreya started
to bounce up and down. "Do you want
to dance?" Shanti said to her.

"Let's all dance!" said Pari. She and
Anvi dragged Shanti to her feet and they
danced along with the music. Soon the
four girls were giggling and falling over.

"We'll dance at the wedding, won't we,
Shanti?" exclaimed Pari.

"Yes. There'll be lots of dancing—
oh!" Shanti broke off with a gasp as
an idea popped into her head. Rekha
hadn't planned any entertainment at
the sangeet – well, maybe that could
be her wedding present! She and her

cousins could do a special dance for Rekha! It wouldn't cost anything and Rekha would be delighted. "I've got an idea!" she told her cousins. "How about we work out a dance routine to do at the sangeet on Saturday? We could use the music from one of Rekha's favourite Bollywood films and copy some of the moves. She'd love it!"

"Yes! Yes!" Pari and Anvi cried.

Shreya beamed as she jigged. "Me dance!"

Shanti hurried to the DVD cabinet and pulled out Rekha's favourite movie, *Devdas*. "We'll do the famous dance from this movie. We won't be able to do all

the moves, because some of them are too difficult, but we can make up our own moves for those bits."

"Let's start practising!" said Pari.

Shanti grabbed the controller and forwarded the film to the start of the dance she knew Rekha loved. It was the whole reason her sister had signed up for the Indian dance class where she'd met Ansh! "OK, here we go!"

Shreya was a bit young to learn the dance, but Pari and Anvi tried to copy Shanti's moves as she planned their dance. Shanti had been going to ballet classes since she was little and she'd watched Rekha dance lots of times, so

she didn't find it too hard to come up with a routine. She knew Rekha wouldn't care if it wasn't technically perfect, she'd just be happy that Shanti had tried. *This is the best gift!* Shanti thought happily as she turned the volume up and they repeated the steps they'd just been practising. *Rekha will love it!*

"What is going on in here?" Nani's voice cut in over the music.

Shanti froze. Oh no! She shouldn't have turned the music up so loud. Now they were going to be told off! "I'm sorry, Nani!" She ran to the controller and turned the volume down. She turned round, expecting to see Nani looking

cross, but to her surprise Nani was shaking her head. "No, Shanti. Turn it up!" And putting her hands above her head, she waggled her bottom and shimmied into the living room!

Chapter Six

Shanti's mouth dropped open as Nani danced towards her. "You did not tell me you liked to dance, Shanti," said Nani.

"I love to dance," said Shanti. "I go to ballet and tap classes but I'm not very good at this kind of dancing." She motioned towards the TV. "I haven't

learnt how to do Bollywood dancing."

"Then I shall teach you," said Nani.
"You as well," she said, nodding to the
cousins. "When I was younger, there was
no one who could dance like me."

Shanti could hardly believe it. "Nani,
would you be able to help us plan
a dance for the sangeet?" she asked
eagerly. "I'd really like to do a dance for
Rekha. I thought the cousins and I could
dance together and then perform it as a
surprise."

Nani smiled at her. "That is a very
good idea. Yes, I will help. It shall be our
secret." She flashed Shanti a sudden smile
and went to shut the door. "Now, show

me what you have got so far . . ."

For the next half hour, Nani helped Shanti and the little ones choreograph a dance that they could all do. The time flew by and Shanti felt a flash of disappointment when she heard Auntie Nisha calling from the hall, "Girls! Time to go!"

"But we haven't finished planning the dance," Shanti said.

"You and I can carry on working on it," said Nani, patting her hand. "I will teach you a solo you can do while the little ones do the steps we have just been learning. We will go to my bedroom where we will not be seen."

So, after she'd said goodbye to the cousins, Shanti went up to the spare room where her grandmother was staying. Nani taught her some more moves and showed her how to use her facial expressions to add to the story she was telling with her hands and feet.

"Good, Shanti!" she said approvingly when Shanti performed the whole dance from start to finish for her. "Very good. You obviously take after me. You use your face and body very well." Shanti felt a warm glow as she saw the look of pride on Nani's face. "But I bet you cannot do this," Nani added, her eyes twinkling.

Nani struck a pose with her body slightly turned to one side, her chin up and her arms held out to the front. Humming the music, she stamped her feet rhythmically while performing graceful arm movements to the side and above her head. Then she started to spin, slowly at first but getting faster and faster. Suddenly, she overbalanced!

"Nani!" gasped Shanti, leaping forward and grabbing her grandmother before she could fall. She and Nani clutched each other and staggered for a moment before falling on to the bed. Shanti sat up, her eyes wide. Nani was facing away from her, and her sides

were heaving. She was making strange
wheezing noises.

Oh no, was she hurt?

"Nani!" cried Shanti.

Relief flooded through her as Nani
turned towards her and Shanti realised
that the wheezing noise was laughter.

"It seems your nani isn't as nimble as
she once was!" Nani gasped, clutching
her sides as tears of merriment rolled
down her wrinkled cheeks. "Oh, dearie
me! I must have looked very silly!"
Giggles bubbled up inside Shanti and the
next moment, she was laughing too.

There was a knock on the door. "Is
everything OK in here?" Mum said,

opening the door and poking her head in. She blinked in surprise as she saw Nani and Shanti, chuckling together on the bed.

"We are fine," Nani told her. She patted Shanti's knee. "I am just having fun with my youngest granddaughter."

"Right, great," said Mum, looking slightly stunned. Nani and Shanti grinned at each other as Mum left the room.

"I should go and help lay the table for supper," said Shanti, getting up.

"Good girl," Nani said. "And later you practise and practise. Yes?"

"Yes, Nani," promised Shanti.

Nani nodded approvingly. "And then you can show me your ballet. Maybe you can turn your nani into a ballerina. What do you say, Shanti? We will teach each other!"

Shanti beamed. "I'd really like that!"

She left the room and ran down the stairs, her heart feeling so much lighter. It seemed Nani didn't dislike her, after all. Behind the sharp tongue there was a kind and funny person. Her friends had been right – she and Nani had just needed to get to know each other better. And the best thing was that she now had a wedding gift for Rekha! She couldn't wait to tell the others. *I'll need to practise every moment I can*, thought Shanti. *It's only a few days until the sangeet!*

After supper, when Shanti had got into her pyjamas, she started to practise the dance steps. A knock on her bedroom door interrupted her. She quickly jumped into bed and picked up a book. "Yes?"

Rekha opened the door. "Hey, can I come in a moment?"

"Sure," said Shanti.

Rekha came in and sat on the edge of Shanti's bed. She held her hands over her face and sighed.

"Are you OK?" asked Shanti.

"Not really. They're driving me crazy!" Rekha said. "Mum, Nani, Auntie Nisha . . . It's been fuss, fuss, fuss all day. They want to know everything down to the last detail. Nani's even been going through the menus." She imitated Nani's voice. "What kind of menu is this, Rekha? There's no fruit chaat, no dahi bhalla. What will people say?" She groaned. "I know Ansh wanted a big wedding, but I'm beginning to think we should have eloped!"

"You don't mean that," said Shanti. "It'll be great and you'll really enjoy it. Just think how nice it will be to have all

your family and friends there – and how happy Ansh will be. It's going to be so much fun, Rekha. It honestly is. I can't wait to be your bridesmaid!"

Rekha smiled. "Yeah, I guess you're right. And of course I'm very pleased you're going to be my bridesmaid. There isn't anyone else I would rather have than you." Her eyes met Shanti's. "You know, I'm really going to miss just being able to come and talk to you, Shanti," she added softly.

Shanti swallowed. "I'll miss you too." *More than you know,* she added in her head. "I wish we could have watched *Dance Off* tonight," she said out loud.

Rekha smiled. "It's not too late. We can watch it on catch up now if you want?"

"Oh, yes!" said Shanti. She jumped out of bed and they went to Rekha's room. They climbed into her double bed together and pulled the duvet up like they always did.

Remember this moment, Shanti thought to herself as the theme tune started to play. She glanced across at her sister and at the exact same moment Rekha looked at her. Their eyes met and they both smiled.

Chapter Seven

The rest of the week flew by in a whirl of wedding preparations. On Friday, the family decorated the house and a big tent was put up in the garden for the sangeet. Early on Saturday morning, the three professional mehndi artists arrived and set up a workstation in

the conservatory. Music played and they began work on Rekha's mehndi straightaway, starting with her feet.

A little while later Auntie Nisha and various other cousins and relatives arrived, along with some of Rekha's close friends. As the house filled up with people, Shanti waited eagerly for her friends to arrive. They were sleeping over and she couldn't wait to see what they thought of all the celebrations.

"Oh, wow!" Cora gasped as Shanti opened the door.

"I love your outfit!" said Sophie.

"Really?" Shanti said hopefully. She had put on one of the salwar kameez

that Nani had brought her from India.

"You look amazing!" said Emily.

Shanti smiled. She hadn't been sure about wearing the salwar kameez but Nani had been so helpful with the dance that she had decided to put it on, knowing that it would make her grandmother very happy. The silk tunic top was a deep pink with gold embroidery around the neck and edges and the baggy trousers that fitted tight around her ankles were white with more gold embroidery. When Shanti had looked at herself in the mirror, she'd been surprised by how much she liked how it looked. It was very comfortable, too.

"Come in," she said. "Mum and my aunties are getting the food ready in the kitchen. I'll show you where the mehndi's happening, although we'll have to wait a bit for our turn."

"Is it really OK for us to have it done?" said Emily. "It's not just for the bride?"

"No, it's for anyone who wants it," said Shanti. "Though we won't get anything like as much as Rekha will. She's being done first — it's important her designs have time to dry properly so they don't fade quickly."

"Why?" said Cora. "Doesn't it just need to last for the wedding?"

"Mehndi are more than just pretty

patterns," Shanti said, remembering what Nani had told her when they'd been talking about it the night before over supper. "People believe that the darker the ink and the longer it lasts, the happier the marriage will be. Let's go see how Rekha's getting on."

She took them through to the conservatory. Rekha was sitting in a large chair plumped up with bright cushions. Her feet were up on a footstool and her arms were resting on pillows. Two women were crouched by her feet painting intricate lacy patterns on her skin that looked like peacock tails, while three of Rekha's friends were sitting

around her, watching and chatting. Nani was sitting in another chair, chatting to a third artist in Hindi as she painted a traditional paisley design on the back of one of Nani's hands.

"Hi, guys," Rekha said, smiling. "I'm glad you could come."

"It's really nice of you to invite us," said Sophie.

"Shanti said you're going to have mehndi too but I warn you, it's very boring sitting still for so long," said Rekha. "And it tickles! Why don't you choose what designs you want? There are some books with pictures of designs over there."

"Cool," said Cora, going over and opening up one of the books on the table.

"Have your parents given permission for this, girls?" Nani said, looking over at them sharply.

"My dad said it was fine," said Cora.

"All of you?" said Nani, raising her eyebrows sternly.

Sophie and Emily nodded quickly. "All our parents said it was OK," said Sophie.

"Very good," said Nani with a nod. She started talking in Hindi again.

"Come on. We can come back later. Let's find Mum and see if she needs any help," said Shanti.

"I can see what you mean about your grandma," Cora whispered to her as they left the conservatory. "She is a bit scary."

"I know she seems like that at first, but her bark's worse than her bite," said Shanti. "She's actually really good fun and she's been helping me with the dance I'm going to do for Rekha. Nani loves to dance. She watched all the videos of my ballet shows and even got me to teach her some moves!" She grinned as she remembered teaching Nani how to do pliés and pirouettes. They'd both ended up falling over again!

"Are you nervous about performing the dance tonight?" Sophie asked.

"Terrified!" Shanti admitted. "I've hardly had any time to practise with my cousins. What if it goes wrong? Everyone's going to be watching us."

"It'll be fine," Emily told her. "I'm sure."

"I've got to get my cousins to practise more," said Shanti. "I tried when they arrived but they just want to play." She looked into the lounge where her dad and some of his relatives were pushing the furniture to one side and her little cousins were running around, chasing balloons. Shanti bit her lip. "If they don't practise it's going to be a disaster!"

They went into the kitchen. Various friends and relatives were gathered

around the table arranging finger food on platters and trays.

"Hi, girls!" called Mum.

"Can we help you, Mum?" Shanti asked.

"Yes, please, sweetie. All this food needs to be taken into the conservatory for people to snack on. Then once the kitchen is clear, we can get started on the food for tonight."

Shanti and the others set about carrying the food through and arranging it on the large table that had been set out in the conservatory. There were lots of little savoury snacks – mini samosas, chicken and lamb kebabs – along with

platters of delicious-looking sweets —
barfi, different types of halva in little
bowls, and swirls of fried jalebi with a
sugary glaze. There were also bowls of
crisps and popcorn and strawberries
dipped in chocolate — Rekha's favourite.

"Help yourself," said Shanti, seeing her
friends looking at the food. "Everything's
delicious."

Emily bit into a samosa. "*Mmm* — this
is so yummy!" she said.

"So's this," said Sophie, trying a jalebi.

"Your house looks amazing," said
Cora, glancing round. "I love the gold
decorations."

Shanti felt a flush of pride. The

house looked beautiful and was full of guests of all ages, laughing, chattering and bustling about preparing for the celebrations.

Her friends tucked in to the food and when Nani's mehndi were finished, they took it in turns to sit in the chair to have their hands painted. Shanti decided to have a delicate flower design down her middle finger and across the back of her hands. Sophie's mehndi looked like waves, because she loved swimming. Emily chose flowers and swirls like Shanti, and Cora persuaded the artist to do her a design with horseshoes. Their designs were far less intricate than

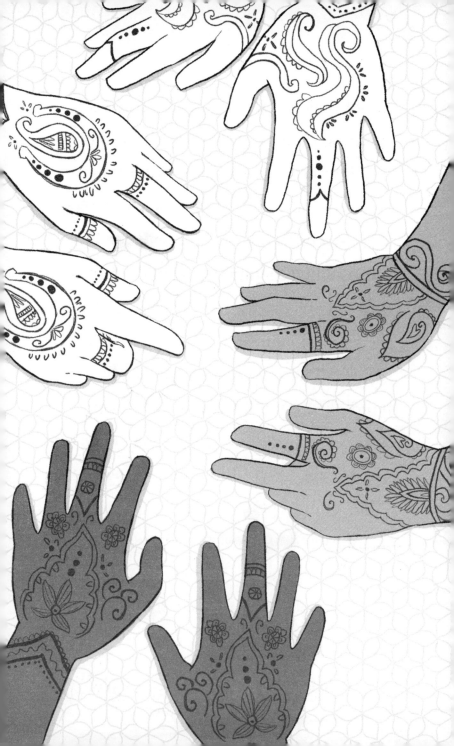

Rekha's so took less time. By the time the four of them were done, Rekha's fingers had only just been started on.

Cora tugged on Shanti's sleeve as they left the conservatory. "While Rekha's busy, why don't you get your cousins to practise the dance?" she whispered.

"Good idea," said Shanti. But when she went into the lounge and asked her cousins to go upstairs with her, they shook their heads.

"We don't want to practise!" said Anvi. "We want to play."

"We already know the dance," said Pari, frowning.

"Not well enough," said Shanti, feeling

worried. "Please come and practise."

Seeing a balloon bouncing on the floor, Shreya giggled and ran after it.

Shanti gave her friends an anxious look. "What am I going to do?" she said as her cousins ran away through the French doors and into the marquee.

"Let me try," said Cora. "Do you know what their favourite sweets are?"

"Coconut barfi, I think," said Shanti. "There's some in the kitchen."

"Can you get me some?" said Cora.

Shanti returned with a bowlful.

"OK, here we go," said Cora. They all went into the marquee, where Cora nibbled on a piece of barfi. "Oh, wow,

this is absolutely delicious!" she said loudly. "Yum!" She took another bite.

"Can we have some?" asked Pari, running over.

"Please?" said Anvi, reaching up for the bowl.

Cora held it high above their heads. "I suppose you can, but you'll have to come and practise the dance." She saw the doubtful look on their faces. "We can have a competition to see who's best," she said persuasively. "Starting now. Whoever gets to Shanti's room first can

have the biggest piece of barfi!"

Pari and Anvi whooped and raced away. "Come on, Shreya!" said Cora, handing the bowl to Shanti and scooping up the little girl. "Let's go! I'm going to fly you up there like you're an aeroplane!"

Shreya shrieked with laughter as Cora carried her inside and up the stairs.

"You're really good with little kids," said Shanti, running after her with Emily and Sophie.

Cora grinned over her shoulder. "I've had loads of practice with my stepsister-to-be."

They crammed into Shanti's tiny

bedroom and gave out pieces of barfi to the younger girls. But there was no space to dance in Shanti's room, so she took them into Rekha's room instead. "She won't mind. She'll be busy with the henna for ages," said Shanti. She found the music on her phone. "OK, let's check you can still remember the moves," she said to her cousins.

But as the music played it was clear her cousins couldn't remember the dance at all! Pari went one way and Anvi went another. When one of them spun round, the other wiggled her hips. When Pari put her arms over her head, Anvi kicked her legs. Shreya didn't even

try and join in – she just ran around the
room pretending to be an aeroplane.
"Crash!" she cried, throwing herself at
the beanbag.

The music came to an end. Pari and
Anvi bumped into each other and fell
over laughing.

Shanti looked at her friends in
despair. "What am I going to do?" she
exclaimed. "The dance is going to be a
complete disaster!"

Chapter Eight

"Don't worry. Why don't we all do the dance together?" said Sophie. "Teach it to us from the start, Shanti. We'll each dance with one of your cousins and help them."

"Come on, everyone," said Cora, clapping her hands. "Let's do it again

and see who's best this time! We'll learn it then we'll see who does it best."

"Can we have more barfi?" asked Anvi.

"Depends how good you are," said Cora, grinning.

Shanti began to teach her friends the dance. They picked it up quickly and soon they were having fun teaching the little ones.

"Come on, Anvi. Show me how to do it," said Sophie. "Do I go this way?"

"No," Anvi giggled. "It's this way, silly!"

"What about this move, Pari?" said Emily. "Do I have to jump like this?"

Pari burst out laughing as Emily did a star jump. "No. You do this!" she said,

showing her the right move.

Cora took Shreya's arms and waved them in time to the music. "We're the best, Shreya!" she said.

Shreya giggled gleefully.

Soon they were all doing the dance together. Sophie, Cora and Emily did

 the backing dance with the younger girls, while Shanti did her solo.

"That was much better," said Shanti.

"Right, guys,

do it again but without us joining in," Cora said to Shanti's cousins.

But to Shanti's dismay, when the older girls didn't join in, the little ones got very confused and forgot the steps.

"What are we going to do?" said Shanti. "They can only do it when you join in."

Just then the door opened and Nani poked her head round it. "What is going on here?"

Shanti groaned. "Oh, Nani. I've been trying to get Pari, Anvi and Shreya to practise the dance for Rekha but it's not going well. It's going to be so bad. I wanted to make Rekha happy, but this is

going to be a dance disaster."

She tensed, waiting for Nani's sharp words, but to her surprise her grandmother came over and patted her arm. "It will be all right, Shanti. You are a very good sister for trying so hard. Rekha will be happy however the dance turns out."

"But I want it to look really good!" protested Shanti.

"Then, let me see what you have," Nani said.

"The girls dance better if we do it with them," said Sophie.

Nani waved a hand. "All together then. Music, Shanti."

They got into position and Shanti pressed 'play'. The music blared out and they started to dance. The practising had worked and even Shanti had to admit they looked pretty slick.

"What is the problem?" said Nani with a shrug as they finished. "You have done an excellent job, Shanti."

"It's fine when Sophie, Emily and Cora are dancing too," explained Shanti. "But when they don't dance, Pari, Anvi and Shreya forget what they're supposed to be doing."

"*Pfff!* So let your friends dance too," said Nani. "You will do that, won't you, girls?"

"Of course," said Emily. "If it helps."

"It would be fun to dance," said Cora.

"Yes, dance with us! Dance with us!" said Anvi and Pari, grabbing the older girls' hands.

"Of course we will, if Shanti wants us to!" said Sophie.

Shanti felt a rush of relief. "Oh, yes please. Thank you!"

"Now, I know what you need," said Nani, her eyes sparkling. "New clothes. Indian clothes."

She bustled off and returned a few minutes later with her arms full of brightly coloured clothes. "Salwar kameez!" she said, triumphantly holding

up the outfits she'd brought for Shanti.

In next to no time, Shanti's friends had changed into their new outfits. Sophie chose a pale pink top covered with delicate gold embroidery and matching trousers. Cora went for a beautiful turquoise top with dark blue trousers and Emily picked an orange top with white and gold trousers.

Nani beamed. "You look beautiful. I shall see you later. Now come with me, little ones, it is time for you to eat," she said, shepherding the younger girls away.

"I feel like a Bollywood superstar," said Cora, spinning round.

"I love how this feels," said Emily,

rubbing her hands on the silky fabric of her trousers.

"I can't wait for this evening!" said Sophie. "I could dance all night wearing this."

Shanti grinned. Her friends looked great in their salwar kameez and they seemed really pleased to be wearing them.

The door opened and Rekha came in. Her face was streaked with tears. She stopped in surprise. "What are you guys doing in here?"

"Sorry. We just needed a bit of space," said Shanti. "Are you all right?"

Rekha bit her lip. "No!" Her face

crumpled. "I'm not all right, Shanti." She started to cry. "I'm not all right, at all!"

"What's the matter?' said Shanti, hurrying to her sister in alarm.

Rekha sobbed. "It's everything! I'm fed up with being told to do this and do that. But mostly, I'm worried, Shanti – what if I'm not ready to get married? Am I doing the right thing? I don't think I want to move out!"

For the briefest of moments, Shanti felt a rush of hope. If Rekha didn't go through with the wedding, nothing would have to change. But then she saw her sister's tear-stained face and knew that she was just feeling stressed out.

Rekha loved Ansh and he made her happy. She should get married – she would be utterly miserable if she didn't.

"Oh, Rekha, you mustn't feel like this," said Shanti, sitting beside her and putting an arm around her sister's shoulders. "Please don't cry. The fuss will be over soon and then it'll be just you and Ansh, being married and living together. That's what you want, I know it is. It's just this wedding fuss giving you cold feet."

Rekha continued to cry. Shanti searched for something to say or do that would comfort her and suddenly came up with the perfect thing. "Look, wait here. I'll be back in a moment."

The rest of the Bridesmaids Club took over comforting Rekha as Shanti hurried to her room and got her mobile phone. She opened her contacts and quickly phoned a number. A few minutes later, she returned to Rekha's bedroom. Shanti's friends were clustered around her, stroking her back.

"I know everyone is fussing, but it's only because they want the day to go really well," said Sophie.

Rekha sniffed.

Seeing Shanti, Sophie made a space for her on the bed next to Rekha.

"It's true. In just a few days the wedding will be over," Shanti said. "And

you'll be living with Ansh. You love him
and he loves you and that's all that
matters."

Rekha looked at her. "You're right,"
she said, giving her sister a watery smile.

"Are you hungry?" said Shanti. "Have
you eaten anything yet?"

Rekha shook her head.

"Why don't we go and fetch
something for you?" said Emily, jumping
to her feet.

"Thanks. Can you get a watermelon
juice, a few samosas, a bowl of halva and
some strawberries?" said Shanti, listing
her sister's favourite foods. Her friends
nodded and left.

Rekha sighed. "Thanks, Shanti," she said, resting her head against Shanti's arm.

For a moment Shanti felt like she was the older sister. "It'll be OK," she said, hugging Rekha tight. "I promise it will be. This wedding is a bit like Nani, you know."

Rekha gave her a confused look. "What do you mean?"

"Well, Nani nags and scolds and can be annoying, but it's only because she loves us. The wedding is kind of the same. I know everyone seems to be pestering you at the moment and it all feels a bit much. But you've got to remember, it's

just their way of showing how much they love you."

Rekha stared at Shanti for a moment and then a small smile pulled at her lips. "You're right." She shook her head. "You're pretty smart, Shanti."

Shanti grinned. "Well, I've always been the clever one of the family!"

Rekha gave her a playful push. "The cheeky one, you mean!"

There was a scraping sound outside the window. Rekha frowned and looked round. "What was that?"

"I really don't know," said Shanti, trying to look innocent, although she had a pretty good idea what it was.

"Why don't you go and have a look?"

Rekha went over to the window. Just as she reached it, a familiar smiling face popped up outside.

Rekha gasped as her groom-to-be, clinging to the top of a ladder, grinned at her through the glass!

Chapter Nine

"Ansh! What are you doing?" Rekha exclaimed. She pushed the window up. "Be careful! You could fall!"

"Better let me in then," said Ansh, his eyes twinkling. "Hi, Shanti," he said, as Rekha helped him over the window ledge and into the room.

"I don't understand," Rekha said, looking dazed. "What are you doing here? You're not supposed to be at the mehndi."

"I know, but a certain little bird," Ansh winked at Shanti, "rang me and told me you were upset so I decided to come and see you. I couldn't come in through the front door, of course, so I brought a ladder and here I am!"

"Oh, Ansh!" breathed Rekha. "I love you." She stepped forward into his arms and the next moment they were kissing.

When they pulled apart, Rekha started running her hands through her hair. "Ugh, I look terrible. I've been

crying so much my make-up has run. You shouldn't see me like this – I'm a complete mess!"

"You always look beautiful to me," Ansh said, using his finger to wipe away the smudges of mascara. "But I hate the thought of you crying. Look, if this whole wedding thing is too much we can always elope. We can go now, just the two of us. I know I was all about the big wedding, but the most important thing is that we get married – and that you're happy."

"Oh, Ansh!" Rekha pulled him close. "That is so sweet. But we can't elope now. Shanti's made me see that the fuss

is because everyone loves us and wants our wedding day to be perfect. Also," she pulled a face, "do you know how many hours I've had to sit still to get this mehndi done? There is no way I'm eloping without a chance to show it off!" She grinned and wiggled her fingers so he could admire her henna designs. "Seriously, it means the world to me that you would be willing to elope, but it's only a couple of days. Soon it will all be over and we'll be together, just the two of us, for the rest of our lives."

Shanti felt a rush of relief.

"Then a big wedding it is," Ansh said. He rumpled Shanti's hair fondly.

"Thanks for ringing me and telling me to come, Shanti."

Rekha smiled too. "Yes, I feel much happier now." She glanced in her mirror. "I guess I'd better re-do my make-up and get ready for the sangeet though."

Ansh nodded. "Cool. I'll see you later." He went to the door.

"Ansh!" Rekha exclaimed. "What are you doing? You can't go out that way. Everyone will freak if they know you've been here."

"Guess I'd better leave the way I came in then!" Ansh grinned as he went over to the window. "Bye, babe. See you both at the sangeet!"

He swung himself out and disappeared. Rekha turned to Shanti. Her eyes were shining. "You're the best sister ever. You do know that, don't you?"

Shanti grinned. "I do my best!"

After Ansh's visit, Rekha was much more cheerful. She got ready for the sangeet and a few hours later, people started arriving. The mehndi artists had gone home, the trays of finger food had been cleared away and the dining room table was groaning under the weight of food for the sangeet – creamy butter

chicken, a variety of fruity chutneys, cool yoghurt, fluffy pilau rice, garlic naan bread as well as delicious spicy snacks – paneer lollipops and little kebabs. Music was playing and as people arrived, they were ushered through to the marquee where there was a dance floor as well as padded, white-and-gold thrones for Ansh and Rekha to sit on.

Rekha looked beautiful in the lehenga she had chosen for the night. The long skirt was made of a heavy, deep pink silk with gold embroidery around the hem and up the skirt to the waist. The matching choli – a cropped, close-fitting top – had a scoop neck edged with gold

and sleeves that came to her elbows.

"Do you like it?" she said, doing a twirl as Shanti and the rest of the Bridesmaids Club came over.

"You look beautiful!" Shanti said and the others nodded.

"Like a princess!" said Sophie.

When Ansh arrived with his friends and family, he had changed into a cream-and-gold outfit. All the other guests were wearing bright, lavish clothes too and Shanti suddenly felt very happy. Her salwar kameez felt completely right for the occasion. Her friends seemed to love theirs, too, and different aunties kept giving them compliments about how

nice they looked.

Oh, I hope the dance goes well, thought Shanti, butterflies fluttering in her tummy as she looked at her sister greeting Ansh's family.

"Welcome, everyone," said Rekha, leading them into the house.

"Babe, it's been so long since I saw you last," said Ansh with a mischievous twinkle in his eye as he kissed Rekha.

She grinned, playing along. "It really has been ages, hasn't it?"

Shanti bit back a giggle.

More and more people arrived until it felt like not a single extra person could fit into the marquee. Drinks were handed out – delicious watermelon coolers and refreshing mango smoothies, as well as creamy cocktails. The noise level rose as people ate and talked, but there was a hush as Rekha walked on to the dance floor. Everyone watched as she danced for Ansh and then they all began to join in.

Shanti felt a tug on her sleeve. It was Pari. "When are we dancing, Shanti?"

"Soon," Shanti said, feeling a rush of nerves. She waited until Rekha took a break from dancing and then whispered to her friends. "Should we do it now?"

Sophie nodded. "We'll go and ask the DJ to put the music on."

Shanti went over to her sister. Rekha was mopping her forehead and laughing with Ansh.

"Rekha," Shanti said, biting her lip. "I've got a surprise for you."

"Ooh, what is it?" said Rekha.

"Well, I didn't have any money to buy you a present so I tried to think of something I could do that you would really like. We both love dancing and you and Ansh met at a dance class . . ."

Rekha's eyes widened. "You're going to do a dance?" she broke in. "Here? For me?"

Shanti nodded quickly. "I wanted to do something special."

"Oh, Shanti!" Rekha burst out. She hugged her tightly. "Is it a ballet dance?"

"No, it's a Bollywood dance," said Shanti.

Rekha squealed. "Oh, Shanti! This is amazing! I can't wait to watch you."

"It's not just me," said Shanti quickly. "It's Sophie, Emily and Cora, plus Pari, Anvi and Shreya. We're all going to dance together."

She looked round. Sophie was standing beside the DJ desk and Emily and Cora were rounding up the little girls. This was it! The moment had come! Shanti nodded to Sophie, who spoke to the DJ and the familiar music came on.

"Ooh! It's from *Devdas!*" cried Rekha, recognising the song. "My favourite."

Trying not to think how nervous she was, or about how everyone was watching her, Shanti ran to the centre of the dance floor. "This is a dance for Rekha!" she called.

Nani clapped her hands in delight. "Entertainment time! Everyone watch my talented youngest granddaughter."

Rekha clapped joyfully. "Go, Shanti!"

For a moment, Shanti felt scared as everyone in the marquee stopped what they were doing to watch, but then the rest of the Bridesmaids Club came running on to the dance floor, each holding the hand of one of her little cousins.

Hearing the melody playing out of the speakers, Shanti knew there was no going back. She struck her opening pose – hands up, fingers pointing out – and then she began to dance. She moved her body to the music, blocking out everything else as she lost herself in the rhythm. As she spun around, stamped

her feet and wiggled her hips, she remembered what Nani had taught her and used her face as expressively as she could. Soon she forgot about the people watching her and the only thing she was aware of were her friends and cousins, dancing with her.

Pari and Anvi were brilliant, adorably copying Sophie and Emily's moves. Shreya tried to wander off but Cora picked her up, swaying and twirling in time with the music. Shreya giggled in delight. "Me dance! Me dance!" she shrieked happily.

Shanti began to dance her solo, hopping on one leg and spinning around

and around. She finished with a flourish, down on her knees with her hands in the air, as the others posed beside her.

Everyone clapped and whooped. There was so much noise that Shanti thought the marquee's roof would come off. She looked over at her sister and saw that Rekha's eyes shone with tears. Ansh was beside her, his arm around her shoulders.

Shanti went over to them shyly. "Did you like it?" she asked Rekha.

"No – I loved it!" said Rekha, one hand on her heart. "Oh, Shanti, it meant so much that you did a special dance."

"I really wanted to make you happy," said Shanti.

"And you did," said Rekha. Tears fell down her cheeks. "Oh, Shanti, what would I do without you?"

Shanti felt an overwhelming wave of sadness and swallowed, trying to get rid of the lump that came to her throat. "I guess you're going to find out tomorrow."

Rekha stroked Shanti's hair. "I've been so busy with all the wedding prep, I haven't really thought about that, but you're right. I can't believe I'm moving out tomorrow. I'm going to miss you so much!"

"Don't cry!" begged Shanti. "Tonight's supposed to be a celebration." She forced herself to smile. "And you'll wreck your

make-up again and get told off by Nani and Auntie Nisha if you cry!"

Rekha took a breath.

"Come on," said Shanti, taking her hand. "We've still got one more night before you're married. So let's enjoy it together."

Rekha smiled as she met Shanti's eyes and let her sister lead her on to the dance floor.

Chapter Ten

The sangeet continued long into the night. There was lots more dancing – Ansh's uncles danced for everyone and then his mum and her friends got up too.

"I liked your dance the best though," Rekha whispered to Shanti afterwards.

Eventually, Shanti and the rest of

the Bridesmaids Club were shepherded upstairs by Shanti's mum. "The party's going to go on for a while, but I think you should try and get some sleep. Tomorrow's going to be a long day."

They snuggled down in sleeping bags in Shanti's room, squished in like sardines. The girls usually stayed up talking when they had a sleepover but they were all so tired, they were asleep in minutes, despite the loud music and chatter coming from downstairs.

Early the next morning, Shanti was woken up by Rekha, shaking her gently by the shoulder. "Shanti, you have to get up," she whispered. "We need to start the

ceremonies." Shanti yawned and got out of bed. It was still dark outside. Her mum had told the rest of the Bridesmaids Club yesterday that they could sleep in. The first ceremonies of the day were for the family only.

Rekha had brought up a tray of pastries, fruit and orange juice for the others when they woke up. She shut the door behind Shanti. "Before we go downstairs, there's something I want you to see," she said. She put her hands over Shanti's eyes.

"What are you doing?" Shanti asked, giggling.

"It's a surprise. Follow me!"

Unable to see, Shanti let Rekha guide her a few steps down the corridor. "Ta da!" Rekha said, taking her hands away.

Shanti found herself looking at Rekha's bedroom door. "What's the surprise— Oh!" she gasped.

On the bedroom door, the golden plaque with Rekha's name had been replaced with a new plaque. It said

"Shanti" in sparkly letters.

Rekha smiled at the astonished expression on Shanti's face. "I want you to have

my room now that I'm moving out. It's much bigger than yours."

"Thank you!" said Shanti, hugging her.

"I'm going to leave my TV here too," said Rekha. Shanti's eyes widened. "On one condition," she added. "You've got to let me come back every Monday so we can watch *Dance Off* together. Is it a deal?" She held out her hand.

"Deal," said Shanti eagerly, shaking it.

Rekha smiled. "Thank you so much for the beautiful dance you did yesterday, Shanti, and for getting your friends to perform too."

Shanti grinned happily. "I couldn't have done it without them!"

"It was the best bit of the whole night," said Rekha.

"Even better than when Ansh kissed you?" said Shanti, giving her sister a teasing look.

"Even better!" Their eyes met. Rekha's were shining with emotion. "I love Ansh so much, Shanti, you know I do. I am really glad I'm marrying him, but I love you too. You're my sister and nothing will ever come between us, I promise."

"I promise too," Shanti said softly and they hugged.

"OK," said Rekha, taking a deep breath as they pulled apart. "Are we ready for this?"

"I am, if you are!" Shanti declared.

They went downstairs and the ceremonies started. After the family had gathered, Rekha was given a set of colourful bangles by her uncle and then it was time for the haldi ceremony. Rekha's mum, Nani and the aunties rubbed a special paste on Rekha's face, hands and feet. There was a lot of laughing and arguing about where they should start with the paste.

"Head to toe! Not toe to head!" Nani kept scolding. "Does the younger generation know nothing?"

Shanti went to see if Emily, Sophie and Cora were awake and invited them

to join in. They came down in their pyjamas.

"What's that stuff for?" asked Cora, looking at the thick yellow haldi paste.

"To make Rekha's skin glow," said Mum.

"Try some," said Auntie Nisha, reaching out and blobbing a bit on Cora's nose.

"Now you'll have a nose that glows!" Shanti said with a grin as Cora squealed.

"Everyone can try the haldi," said Nani, scooping some up and rubbing it on her forehead. "There's plenty to go round. Come on, girls! Join in!"

They scooped the paste out of the

bowl and began to chase each other round with it, trying to smear it on each other's faces. A lot of it went on to their pyjamas!

Rekha scrubbed off the haldi, then left to go to the temple. Shanti and the others helped clear up the house and then Sophie had a good idea.

"Maybe you should make a bridesmaid emergency kit. My Auntie Allie had one at my mum and dad's wedding."

They tried to think of everything that might be useful and packed a small silk bag with safety pins, tissues, a little mirror, mascara, some make-up remover

wipes in case Rekha's make-up smudged, concealer and hairspray. "And last but not least, I'll put these in!" said Shanti, holding up something red, soft and flat.

"What are they?" asked Cora.

"Foldable shoes!" said Shanti with a grin. "There's going to be even more dancing today and I bet Rekha's feet are going to get sore."

"You really are the perfect bridesmaid," said Emily.

Shanti glowed. "And you've all been the perfect bridesmaid helpers," she said. "Thank you for coming and helping with the dance and the food and just being here with me."

"It's been brilliant fun," said Emily. "I can't wait to see the rest of the wedding celebrations today."

Rekha came back from the temple and after she had showered, she started having her make-up and hair done. Meanwhile, the girls got into their wedding outfits. Emily, Sophie and Cora wore their salwar kameez again, while Shanti put on her special bridesmaid lehenga. Her mum brushed out her hair until it gleamed, then fixed it to one side with a gold clip and gave her some pretty bangles to wear.

"Oh, wow, you look amazing!" said Sophie when Shanti came back in to

see them. The embroidered pink skirt
reached to the ground. It had a blue
waistband, an orange hem and delicate
gold embroidery all over it.

"I wonder what Nani will think?"
Shanti said nervously.

"Let's go and show her," said Cora.

They went downstairs. When Nani
turned and saw Shanti, her face lit up.

"How do I look, Nani?" Shanti asked
shyly.

"You look beautiful, Shanti," Nani
declared. Then she winked. "I have
changed my mind about bridesmaids –
you will make the perfect bridesmaid for
your sister."

Shanti grinned at her. "Thanks, Nani."

Nani's voice softened. "I was very proud of you last night, Shanti. The dance you did for your sister made her very happy." She gently pinched Shanti's

cheek. "We must continue to get to know each other better. Maybe next year, you would like to come to India and stay with me? You can see the sun, eat the food, meet more of your family, yes?"

Happiness bubbled through Shanti. "Yes, please. I'd love to!"

Nani winked. "Then I shall make it happen."

Shanti hugged her.

"Hi, everyone." Hearing Rekha's voice they turned and everybody caught their breath.

"Oh, wow!" Shanti gasped.

Rekha looked stunning. She was wearing a deep red wedding lehenga. The full skirt had sparkling gold beads sewn on all over it and the hem was heavily embroidered. Her choli had short capped sleeves, showing off the bangles that covered her arms, and a matching red-and-pink scarf was attached to a comb in her hair and fell down her back.

"You look like a Bollywood movie star!" exclaimed Shanti. It was true – her sister looked incredibly glamorous. As well as her bangles, she wore a thick gold choker with a large ruby in the centre of it, and two longer necklaces. She had a diamond nose ring, heavy gold earrings and a large glittering pendant sat in the centre of her forehead. Her eyes had been made up with lots of eyeliner and her skin really did seem to glow.

Mum, the aunties and Nani fussed around Rekha, feeling the fabric of her skirt, admiring the fineness of her jewellery, exclaiming over her make-up. Shanti watched anxiously, hoping

Rekha would be OK with the fuss. But her sister smiled and laughed, her nerves seemingly vanished.

Shanti felt a rush of relief. She had wanted Rekha to have the best wedding day ever and now it looked like it might actually happen!

Chapter Eleven

They all piled into taxis and headed to a nearby banquet hall where the actual wedding was taking place. Drummers were playing Indian drums to welcome the wedding guests into a huge room where a pink stage had been set up with four pillars draped with deep pink-and-

silver silk cloths and a bright red canopy.

"Oh, it's so pretty!" exclaimed Shanti, looking around. Garlands of roses, jasmine and lilies decorated the pillars and a curtain made of strings of fairy lights sparkled at the back of it. There were steps leading on to the stage and in between the pillars there were low golden benches with pink-and-red cushions and a bowl of fire.

Lots of guests had already arrived and the atmosphere was warm and welcoming. Some people were dressed in traditional Indian dress, while others were wearing suits and brightly coloured dresses and skirts. Everyone was smiling

and laughing as they chatted and then the drums began playing even more loudly.

"What's happening?" asked Cora.

"It's Ansh and his family – they're here for the jaan!" said Shanti, looking out of a window. "Come on!" They hurried to the entrance.

Ansh rode up to the hotel on a white horse with a crowd of his family and friends making a noisy procession around him. They were greeted warmly by Rekha's family, who welcomed them inside.

"Now it's time for the wedding ceremony to begin," Shanti told her

friends. "I'd better go be a bridesmaid!"

"Good luck!" Emily said, and they all gave her a hug.

Ansh went to wait by the stage and then Rekha appeared. Walking into the room behind her sister, Shanti knew she would never forget the expression on Ansh's face. He looked spellbound, lost for words. His eyes met Rekha's and they both smiled, as though they were the only two people in the room.

The bride and groom were handed garlands of flowers, which Shanti knew were called haar. Rekha had to try and get her garland over Ansh's head while everyone clapped and cheered her on.

He teased her, ducking and dodging as if he wanted to avoid the flowers going over his head. Finally, she caught him. As the garland landed round his neck, he caught her hands and smiled. "Just joking," he said.

"You'd better be!" she said back, her eyes sparkling.

After that, Shanti lost track of everything that happened – there was chanting from the wedding priest conducting the ceremony, Ansh drinking from a bowl of water and sprinkling it on his feet, Rekha's father and mother giving her away and then Ansh and Rekha walked around the fire several

times. Ansh put red powder on Rekha's forehead and a necklace of gold-and-black beads over her head and finally, the main marriage ceremony was over.

"We're married," Rekha declared. "Now it's time to party!"

There was dancing and singing and everyone helped themselves to the delicious buffet.

"I think samosas are my new favourite food," said Cora happily, helping herself to another spicy vegetable-filled pastry.

"I don't know," said Emily, biting into a vegetable fritter. "These pakoras are even yummier."

Rekha and Ansh went to change

into different outfits before cutting the
wedding cake.

When the bride and groom came
back downstairs, Mum began to usher
everyone towards a small room off to the
side where the wedding cake had been
put to keep it safe. "This way! This way!
It's time for the cake, everyone!"

Sophie patted her tummy. "I'm not
sure I can eat anything else . . ."

"Just wait till you see the cake," Shanti
said to her friends as they followed Mum,
Rekha and Ansh. "It's amazing! It's the
same red–and–gold colour as Rekha's
wedding outfit and it's enormous – five
tiers." But just as they reached the room

they heard a loud *CRASH!*

Mum rushed into the room and, after exchanging alarmed glances, the Bridesmaids Club friends followed. They almost bumped into Mum as she stopped in her tracks.

Shanti gave a horrified gasp as she saw what had caused the crash.

Shreya was holding the edge of the tablecloth in her hand and the top layers of the cake were lying in pieces on the floor.

"Oh no!" exclaimed Shanti. "She must have grabbed the tablecloth and pulled the cake over!"

"Me got cake!" Shreya announced

happily, picking up
a big piece with
red-and-gold icing
and waving it at
everyone. "Pretty
cake."

Rekha gasped, her hand flying to
her mouth. Ansh put his arm round her
shoulders.

Mum's face crumpled and she burst
into tears.

"Oh, Shreya, no! You naughty, naughty
girl!" exclaimed Auntie Nisha, rushing to
scoop up her youngest daughter. "I'm so
sorry, Rekha!"

"The cake is ruined!" said Mum.

"Whatever are we going to do?"

Shanti glanced at Rekha. To her relief her sister had seen the funny side. She and Ansh were giggling.

"Don't worry, Mum," Rekha said. "It's just a cake and everyone's had more than enough to eat!"

"But it's your wedding cake!" cried Mum. "You're supposed to cut it and then we hand it round."

"Now, now, Rekha is right," said Nani, bustling forward and putting an arm around Mum. "The cake is on the floor, so what? Do not cry now. What is one cake when we have all this!" She swept her hand round. "Family, friends, a happy couple." She wagged a finger at Mum. "You worry too much about everything being perfect, Ramnik."

"I do?" said Mum, her surprise making her stop crying.

Nani nodded. "Yes. You should relax more," she said with a shrug. "You have two daughters you should be proud of – they are kind, clever girls. And I am proud of *you* for being such a good mother."

"Oh, Maa." The next moment, Mum was hugging Nani. As they embraced, Shanti exchanged delighted smiles with Rekha. Nani was right – who cared about the cake?

"Now, come!" Nani said as she and Mum pulled apart. "Let us stop worrying about the cake and start dancing!"

Nani twirled around, clapping her hands in time to the music. Soon, everyone was up on the dance floor. Shanti and her friends danced until their feet were sore and it was time for Rekha and Ansh to leave.

Before Rekha got into the car that was taking her and Ansh to a hotel for their honeymoon, she broke away and ran over to Shanti who was standing with the rest of the Bridesmaids Club. "Promise me, you'll be waiting for me next Monday to watch *Dance Off.*"

"I promise," said Shanti, hugging her sister hard.

As Rekha got into the smart white car, Cora, Emily and Sophie clustered around Shanti. Rekha and Ansh waved through the back window as the car began to drive away.

"Are you OK?" Sophie asked Shanti.

Shanti nodded. She had tears in her eyes but she didn't feel as sad as she had expected. "I am." She glanced across at where Nani was arm-in-arm with Mum. "I've been dreading Rekha moving out, but it doesn't really matter if you live apart from your family. Rekha might be moving out, but she'll always be my

sister. Her getting married won't change that. Family is family, no matter where you live."

Emily hugged her. "And friends are friends wherever they are too."

Shanti grinned. "That's true. Thank you all for helping me to be Rekha's bridesmaid. I couldn't have done it without you."

"We didn't do much," said Cora.

"You were there when I needed you," said Shanti. "And that made all the difference."

They smiled at each other.

"You're going to be the next bridesmaid, Cora," said Emily.

"In a posh, fairy-tale castle," said Sophie.

Cora sighed. "A fairy-tale castle complete with a wicked stepmother."

"It'll be amazing," said Shanti, taking her friend's hand. "The Bridesmaids Club will make sure of it."

"Because that's what we're here for!" said Sophie.

"No matter what!" declared Emily.

"Girls! Girls! Come inside!" called Nani, beckoning to them. "There is plenty more food to eat and more dancing to be done."

Linking arms, the Bridesmaids Club headed back inside, to where the music

was blasting out, the guests were dancing and love – and the delicious scent of samosas – was in the air!

The End

Save the date!

Read on for a sneak peak of Cora's story . . .

Cora finished brushing Star's silky mane and hugged him, breathing in the sweet smell of pony. Outside, in the stable yard, she heard a car horn beep for the second time. Reluctantly, she put the brush away in her grooming box. Star nudged her with his nose, looking for treats.

Cora rummaged in her pockets and found a couple of pony cubes. They were a bit old and fluffy but Star didn't mind. He snaffled them from her open palm, the whiskers on his muzzle tickling her skin. Cora kissed him.

BEEP . . . BEEP!

The car horn sounded even more impatient now. Cora sighed. "I guess

I'm going to have to go before Horrible Helena explodes." She pulled a face. "I wish she would explode and disappear, Star. She's so annoying. I can't believe she's going to be my step-mum."

Star snorted softly.

BEEP . . . BEEP . . . BEEP!

Cora knew she had put off going home for as long as she could. She gave Star a last hug, checked he had enough water and left the stable. She walked slowly over to where the shiny, black car was waiting for her, its engine running. Her dad was sitting in the front passenger seat, Helena was in the driver's seat and behind her sat her five-year-old daughter, Mollie May. Mollie May was chattering to Helena and Dad, her hair a halo of blonde curls around her head.

"You should turn your engine off when you're not driving," Cora said to Helena as she opened the door and got into the back beside Mollie May, her boots and socks shedding straw on to the pristine car mat. "It's really bad for the environment to keep the car engine's running." Her comments were directed at Helena but it was her dad who answered.

"We hadn't realised we'd be waiting here for ten minutes. What took you so long? Didn't you hear the horn?"

"Yeah, I heard it," Cora said. Her dad turned to look at her over his shoulder. For a moment, she thought he would get cross but then he just sighed and turned back to the front. "Right, well let's get going."

"Can we have the music on, Mummy?" asked Mollie May as Helena started to drive away. "Pleeeease!" As usual, she had a princess dress on. She had a whole wardrobe of them, along with a shelf of tiaras and sparkly shoes. Today, she was dressed as Sleeping Beauty in a frothy, pink dress.

"Of course, sweetie," said Helena, turning the music on. The music from

Frozen filled the car and Mollie May started to warble along.

Cora groaned. "Do we have to listen to this again? Can't we listen to the radio?"

"But this is my favourite!" said Mollie May, her mouth turning pouty as she started to frown.

"Don't I know it!" muttered Cara.

"I want *Frozen*!" said Mollie May, mutinously.

"We can have your choice of music in the car tomorrow, Cora," said Helena. "And Mollie May's today. OK?"

Cora scowled. Why did Mollie May always get first choice? Helena spoilt her rotten. Mollie May started to sing again.

"Dad!" Cora protested, leaning forwards. "We always do whatever Mollie May wants, never what I want. It's not fair!"

"That's not true," said Dad. "Stop being so grumpy, Cora, and join in. You used to like this song."

"Yeah, when I was a baby!" muttered Cora.

"I'm not a baby!" Mollie May protested.

Cora folded her arms and slumped down in her seat as her dad joined in with the song and encouraged Mollie May to sing with him too. He didn't get it. He really didn't understand how much she hated living with Horrible Helena and Mollie May. Just because he loved them didn't mean she did too.

When they'd moved in a few months ago, he'd even said she might like not being an only child any more. But Cora didn't want a little sister, particularly not an annoying one like Mollie May who just wanted to play princesses all the time. And she didn't want a step-mum either, especially not a glamorous, fashion-obsessed one like Horrible Helena who was now joining in with the singing and throwing soppy glances at Dad. *Yuck!*

Cora pulled out her phone to see if

there were any texts from Emily, Shanti
and Sophie. She and Emily had been
best friends ever since they had started
at Cross Hills Primary School but they
had only really got to know Shanti and
Sophie, who were in the other Year Six
class, a few months ago.

The four of them had become friends
when they had discovered they were
all going to be bridesmaids. They had
formed a club – the Bridesmaids Club
– with the aim of helping each other
be the best possible bridesmaids they
could be. They all agreed that being a
bridesmaid wasn't just about wearing a
dress and carrying flowers; bridesmaids

were supposed to help the bride and make sure the wedding ran smoothly.

Sophie had been chief bridesmaid at her mum and dad's wedding. On their fifteenth anniversary of being together, Sophie's dad had proposed. They'd planned to have a wedding abroad but then he'd lost his job and it had looked like the wedding would be called off. However, the Bridesmaids Club had come to the rescue and organised an amazing wedding on the beach at home instead.

Shanti had been her sister Rekha's bridesmaid. Rekha's fiancé, Ansh, had wanted a big traditional Indian wedding and Shanti had been desperate to find the perfect wedding gift to give her sister. The Bridesmaids Club had helped her solve that problem too, by performing a special dance for the bride. The wedding had been brilliant and Rekha had absolutely loved her surprise dance.

The next wedding was going to be Cora's dad's and Helena's. Cora knew her friends thought she should feel more excited about it – it was going to take place in a real-life castle, just like in a fairytale. *It's actually exactly like being in a fairytale,* she thought crossly. *I've got a wicked stepmother and annoying stepsister. I just wish I had a fairy godmother too, one who could grant my wish – of cancelling the wedding!*

There were no messages from her friends when she checked her phone but of course Sophie would still be at her swimming training and Shanti and Emily would only just have finished their ballet class. *I'll text them later*, Cora thought as Helena parked the car in the driveway of their house.

They lived in a large modern house with big windows and a semi-circular driveway in front of it. Cora and her dad had moved there two years ago – a year and a half after her mum had died of cancer. He'd wanted a fresh start, he'd told Cora. She'd wanted to stay in their old house, the terraced house that was full of memories of her mum but that was the problem about being eleven, you didn't get a say in where you lived – or who you lived with. You just had to put up with whatever the adults decided.

To find out what happens next,
read **Fairytale Wedding Wish!**

Have you read **Beach Wedding Bliss** yet?
See where Bridesmaids Club began!